THE GOOD
THE BAD
AND THE
NAUGHTY

THE GOOD, THE BAD, AND THE NAUGHTY

NATALYA

NATALYA WRITES PUBLISHING

I dedicate this book to Yah—my God, my Creator and Sustainer. Without You, I simply wouldn't exist, and through Your grace, all things are possible. This vision is fulfilled, and my dream is realized, because of You.

To my family who loved me through every season, stood by me during the darkest moments, and reminded me who I am when I forgot. You all were my anchor when everything else felt uncertain.

To the special person who came into my life and held me together while I found my way back to myself. Your patience kept me steady even on the hardest days. You came at a time when I needed strength the most, offering unwavering support and a quiet kind of love that gave me the courage to heal, to grow, and to believe in love once again.

To those who came before—thank you for the lessons, which, in the end, became a verse in my story.

To my circle, the ones who saw the vision before the ink touched paper, who whispered "keep going sis" when my spirit whispered stop. My first audience whenever I crafted a new poem, your love and support mean the world to me.

To those who prayed for me—you built a bridge of faith when mine had too many cracks. As it is said, "One plants the seed, another waters it, but God gives the increase."

Every line carries your fingerprints.

Every page remembers your name.

CONTENTS

ACKNOWLEDGEMENTS

I want to express my deepest gratitude to my mom, my children, and their families—whose love and support have been a constant source of joy and strength. Your presence in my life, both near and far, reminds me daily of the beauty and resilience of family. You believed in me before I believed in myself. I love y'all to life!

My heartfelt thanks to my friend and mentor, Shannon Singletary—your wisdom, guidance, and indie writer expertise helped shape this dream into reality. You offered your time so freely and shared your knowledge so selflessly, and for that, I am forever grateful.

I would like to acknowledge Candice Nicole for her exceptional proofreading and steadfast dedication to ensuring the clarity and quality of this manuscript. Your professionalism and care elevated this work in every way.

To everyone who shared your stories and allowed me to give them voice—thank you for your trust, your courage, and your belief in me. From the depths of my heart, I am truly thankful.

THE GOOD

A tender reflection on the end of one love and the surprising arrival of another, "The Good" captures the fragile hope, love, gratitude, small joys, and quiet moments of peace.

ForNever

Go live your life, baby.

This was fun while it lasted.

Like Usher said, *I hate we didn't make it to forever*,

but sometimes life doesn't bend the way we want it to.

Go do your thing, babe. I won't hold you back.

I just pray you don't wake up the love

in another woman

just to leave her wondering what happened.

That shit hurts,

especially when there's no real reason

why such a good man

can be bad at love.

No,

you're good at love.

You're bad at keeping it.

Go live your life, baby.

And if the day ever comes

when you finally learn

how to hold love without letting it slip away,

I hope you remember

someone once prayed for you to get there.

And maybe,

when the silence finds you,

you'll finally understand—

love was never the problem,

holding on to it was.

Now I'm the one letting go,

with tenderness still in my soul

and the quiet ache on my chest

of another broken heart.

Look Deeper

Just like not everything that glitters is gold

Not every smile is happy

Not every tear is sad

Not every helping hand has money

Not every *I love you* goes beyond words

Not every pain is visible.

Through the glitter

Through the tears

Through the drought

Through the lies

Through the pain

I will always thank God because I am still here.

He finds me worthy of another day.

It is said He only gives His toughest battles to His strongest soldiers.

And many times, we don't believe we are strong enough.

But like a parent that teaches their child to ride a bike,

He encourages me and says *"Keep going, baby, you're almost there. I got you. I promise."*

I pick up whatever strength I have left and keep moving.

My Daddy's said I can, so I will.

So, like glitter, I sparkle.

I will have a happy soul and

Shed happy tears.

I will take my blessings and bless others.

I will love everyone just as God has commanded, no matter what.

And through the pain,

By faith and trust in Him,

I SHALL MAKE IT!

Since the First Moment

We met—an instant spark,

Like the universe had whispered our names.

You looked at me and made me feel

As if no other woman had ever existed in the world.

In your arms, I found safety.

A quiet place where I could breathe,

Where my walls could crumble without fear,

Where my heart could finally rest.

You listened—not just to my words

But to the spaces between them,

The unspoken truths I did not know I carried.

With you, love was patient.

It didn't rush; it didn't demand.

It held me steady

When storms rose inside me

And celebrated quietly

In the ordinary moments.

Coffee in the morning,

Your hand brushing mine,

The warmth of your presence

That made everything feel right.

You showed me that love

Isn't a chase or a thrill.

It's a promise kept

Without having to say a word.

And in that love, I became

The fullest version of myself.

Unconditional

In marriage—in love—

There is no perfect math.

It isn't always 100/100.

Some days it's 50/50,

Other days it's 70/30.

Sometimes it leans heavy,

90/10,

Or even falls into silence—

100/0.

Love is the willingness

To carry the weight when the other cannot.

To stand steady when storms bend the walls.

To give, not counting the cost.

To trust that tomorrow

The scales will shift again.

So, take your time—

Find your person.

The one who respects you,

Who shows up in all these seasons,

Who has your back

When you're weary.

Who cheers the loudest

When you rise.

Love is not always even,

But it must always be faithful.

Not always balanced

But always rooted.

Take your time.

Because the right one

Will stay through every season—

Not just the easy ones.

Marriage

It's not about trying to be perfect.

More about living

And learning

And doing better in life.

There is no such thing as a perfect love or

Perfect person or

Perfect relationship.

But there is of trying and showing

That someone can be there

Through it all.

Truthfully,

Loyally and

Wholeheartedly.

It's not about people pleasing.

More about pleasing Yah,

Yourself,

And keeping your word.

And enjoying this thing called life—

What's left of it, at least.

Don't let imperfect people bother you.

Instead, welcome the imperfect individuals

Who understand life happens and

Continue walking with you,

Figuring it out along the way.

Because

It's not about what you did

Or have done

Or will do.

It's more about stepping into this new chapter

And killing it

By doing your best.

Because after all this time,

You know better so

Now you do better,

But still imperfectly you

Even at your best.

A Work in Progress

God is still shaping me—

slowly, patiently,

molding my heart through every trial, every tear, every triumph.

I am perfectly imperfect,

a work in progress carried by divine hands.

I am learning to love wholeheartedly,

to open my soul wide without fear,

to give love unconditionally—

not because I'm flawless,

but because love itself is the greatest healer.

Each step I take, each stumble I face,

each quiet moment of surrender,

is a testament to grace unfolding within me.

I am being refined like gold in fire—

stronger, softer, more radiant.

With every breath, I grow closer

to the love that never fails,

the love that heals, renews, and restores.

A love beyond human understanding—

pure, boundless, and eternal.

As I walk this journey,

embracing the imperfect beauty of my soul,

knowing that I am deeply loved

exactly as I am.

The Good Morning Text

It's the good morning text

that's embedded in my mind,

etched deep enough

to find its way to my heart.

Who sent you?

Everything inside me wants to say God,

because you are what I want—

not just tonight

but every day that follows.

You're what I need—

the quiet pulse beneath my chaos,

the craving I didn't know I had,

the breath that fills my lungs

long after the night fades.

You're more than just my bed.

You're the echo in my silence,

the conversation that pierces my soul,

the warmth behind my thoughts.

Every word you send

feels like a thread pulling me closer,

closer to something I didn't dare to name

but now can't live without.

So, who sent you?

Maybe God.

Or maybe just fate,

writing in texts and heartbeats,

that some mornings

are made for you.

Leading Lady

I don't play background.

I don't wait in shadows

or settle for being somebody's maybe.

I am the headline,

the name lit in neon across his chest,

the show they all come to see.

When he speaks my name,

it rolls like thunder,

heavy with promise,

sweet with possession.

When his hands trace me,

it's not casual—

it's worship.

Every kiss is a claim,

every breath a vow—

I am not part-time.

I am the role of a lifetime.

There's no competition,

no audition line,

no stand-in waiting for a chance.

I am the flame he keeps chasing,

the storm he can't contain,

the soft and the savage wrapped in one.

He calls me his peace,

but I know I'm also his fire.

I set his soul ablaze

and still lay him down gentle,

reminding him—

Kings don't rise without their Queens.

So, don't mistake me

for an understudy,

a side role, a secret.

I am the stage, the script, the curtain call.

I am the encore he begs for

when the lights go low.

Front and center,

undeniable, unstoppable—

I am his leading lady.

Grace in the Breaking

I used to cry asking You to fix it—

to fix him,

to fix us,

to fix the pieces I kept breaking

just to keep us whole.

But You saw what I didn't.

You heard what I ignored.

The lies,

the disrespect,

the soul-draining ache

I called love.

You whispered,

"Be still and know that I am God"

even when my world was shaking.

And I was still.

Broken—but still.

You saw the tears he didn't,

heard the prayers he mocked,

and when I couldn't let go,

You did it for me.

Quietly,

softly.

You pulled me out—

with a strength I didn't know I had.

You let me fall just enough

to find my knees

then lifted me higher

than I'd ever dared to pray for.

Now I see it clearly:

That wasn't love.

That was a lesson.

That was You saving me.

Thank You

for not giving me what I thought I wanted.

Thank You

for releasing me from what looked like love

but felt like survival.

Thank You

NATALYA

for closing that door

so gently

it didn't break me—

just set me free.

No More

I'm done competing for your time,

your love,

your respect.

I'll take the loss,

and I wish you the best.

What I had to offer

was never enough

for you.

But I can walk away

with my head held high,

knowing I did everything

to hold on to us—

to the promises we made,

to the vows we said.

Still, it wasn't enough

for you.

Everything in me believed

this would pass.

NATALYA

It was an affair.

It's done.

I swallowed my pride,

kept my composure,

and even that

wasn't enough

for you.

I have so much love to give—

and it was supposed to be

just for you.

But you didn't want to give the same

just for me.

It's one thing to move on

but another

to slap me in the face

with the truth of what you did.

I'm kind.

But I'm not a fool.

I won't beg to be chosen.

I won't compete for love.

I hurt—

but I'll heal.

For me.

Silent Prayers, Loud Pain

I gave you my heart—

the deepest part of me,

the love that burned the brightest,

the trust I wrapped carefully

around every fragile moment we shared.

But you never saw it.

You never heard the silent pleas

or felt the weight of what I needed most—

attention, care, a presence that said,

I'm here for you, always.

I loved you more than I should have,

cared harder than you deserved,

trusted you beyond reason—

hoping you'd catch me,

only to find your hands empty.

There came a day—

a breaking point—

when I looked at myself and wondered,

Why am I losing my mind over someone who won't fight for me?

Love isn't begging.

It isn't pleading for basic respect,

or waiting for crumbs of affection

to feel like enough.

It's a two-way street,

a shared rhythm

that beats with equal passion.

I refused to be your afterthought,

your option, your nothing.

I wanted to be your everything—

the one you cherish,

the one you choose,

the one who lights your world.

So, I walked away—

not because I stopped loving

but because I learned to love myself enough

to say, *This isn't worth losing me.*

And in that moment,

I left—

no glance over my shoulder,

no second guess.

Just a quiet decision

to finally choose me.

And that was the most powerful thing I ever did.

I Miss You

You ever heard the saying "*Seems like forever*"?

It's an actual thing.

Haven't heard from you in 24 hours,

and it feels like a lifetime.

We used to talk or text every day

since this started—

since we started.

Even if it was small stuff,

it meant something.

"It's good to hear from you, even if about business," I once said.

Now?

I would give anything to hear from you—

even if it was about business.

But it's no longer just that.

I'd give anything

to hear your voice,

to feel that quiet comfort you brought

even through a screen.

NATALYA

I want to know how you're doing.

I want to tell you how I've been holding it together—

or not.

I want to say, simply,

I miss you.

I know you've got your reasons.

I know life gets heavy.

And I understand,

even if it stings a little.

But that doesn't stop the silence

from stretching too long.

Doesn't stop the ache

that shows up

in the middle of a regular-ass Tuesday.

I keep checking my phone.

Stupid, I know.

Still, I check.

Still, I wait.

Not because I expect you to come running,

but because a part of me

hoped I meant enough for you to say you miss me too.

That's it.

No pressure.

Just truth.

Drunk Texting

A drunk mind speaks a sober heart

at least that's what they say.

Yes, they say a lot,

but this time, I think they got it right.

When you're tangled in that vulnerable haze,

deep feelings rise like waves,

surfacing the truths your sober mind

has locked away too tight to say.

You reach for your phone,

the glowing screen

a beacon in the night,

to send a message to the one

who sits, unwittingly,

on the throne of your heart.

All those bottled-up emotions spill out—

words you can't, or rather,

won't say when the world is clear,

when your mind is sharp and sober.

It's funny how you need Johnny, Jack, or Jose

to soften your edges,

to crack open your armor

and reveal the coward inside.

Because when you're sober, your lips whisper one story.

But when you're drunk,

your fingers write another.

M. Jane

I watch and wait,

patient as the sun-warmed fruit,

till she's ripe—

ready to ease the weight of the world

with her gentle, smoky breath.

She drapes me in a velvet haze,

a quiet place where noise dissolves

and only stillness remains—

a sacred sanctuary carved from chaos.

I breathe her in,

this soft surrender,

letting go of all that aches,

all that grinds beneath the skin.

And yet, beneath the calm,

a restless hunger hums—

watching, waiting till she's ready

so I can claim her again,

lose myself in her green embrace.

Oh, damn you, Mary Jane—

how you steal my breath,

consume my senses,

bind me tight in your smoky chains—

a sweet, relentless prison

I never want to escape.

So peaceful and serene.

God, Forgive Me

I'm a God-fearing woman,

but I'm cracked,

more like broken,

and this pain won't quiet down.

Time.

They say it heals.

But how can it when I keep tearing at the scab,

picking at the wound that still bleeds

from the moment you broke me?

You say you're God's vessel, sent to test me.

Maybe I'm here for strength.

If that's true,

then let God use me to show you

how deep the hurt cuts.

How heavy this kind of pain is.

I don't understand you.

Did you even see her coming?

Did you try to stop her?

I forgave the girl.

Not because it's easy,

but because I had to let go

to keep from drowning.

But then she reopened the wounds,

telling me your dick ain't mine,

and you didn't even flinch—

didn't say a word to stop her.

That day haunts me.

I begged God to forgive me

for all the anger I swallowed,

for the nights I cried silent prayers,

for the pieces of me lost in this mess.

He's still working on me,

but some days

this burden feels too heavy to bear.

What's poisoning me

is her pushing,

relentlessly

for a year straight,

NATALYA

while I hold all this rage

locked tight inside.

She talks like she owns my pain—

like she's entitled to my heartbreak.

"That's not yours," she taunted

"I wanna see how fucking long you keep him," she spits.

And still, she walks free,

while I'm left picking up the shards.

Now you expect me

to survive another day?

Come on, baby—

show me some grace,

some truth,

some damn reality.

Because right now,

I'm just a woman,

broken and praying

for a strength I don't feel.

But I will not be the story's end.

I am the hand that turns the page,

the woman who gathers the shards of her broken heart

and makes a crown.

Reborn

I didn't plan the fire.

I just got tired of carrying it all—

your lies, my shame, the dead parts of me

you left behind.

I let it burn.

Quietly.

No speeches, no audience.

Just me and the truth

catching fire together.

I won't say I feel strong yet.

Not every scar has closed.

Some nights, I still reach for you

like a bad habit.

But I pull my hand back.

I breathe.

I stay.

I know now

I was never small.

You just needed me that way.

And I kept folding myself up

just to fit your pockets.

No more.

If I rise, it's slow—

on my own legs,

no borrowed crutches,

no empty promises.

If I laugh, it's real.

If I love again, it's honest—

and only when I want to.

You don't get this version.

You don't even get my name on your tongue.

I walk out barefoot,

smelling of smoke,

heart raw—

but it's mine again.

God-sent

I prayed under hush of midnight,

my whispered hope wrapped in heaven's sigh.

And He answered, not with thunder

but with you—quiet miracle, warm sunrise.

You love me like I'm the only heartbeat

walking this wide and broken world.

Your arms are my sanctuary, your hands

my promise that God remembers my name.

You provide like rivers feed gardens,

steady, patient, spilling over—

a friend when storms bend my branches,

a lover when dawn peeks soft through silk sheets.

You teach me how faith wears a human smile,

how grace moves in footsteps across my floor,

how forever can fit in a breath,

in a touch, in a glance that says *you are mine.*

I am a woman kissed by grace,

held by faith,

and loved like the only dream God refused to keep

for Himself.

He's Different

He's the kind of man who prays before he moves,

who looks at you like you're home

and means it.

Just the sound of his voice makes my spirit lift.

The curve of his smile calms the storm inside me.

And when he laughs—Lord, when he laughs—

it feels like Sunday morning all over again.

To experience him is beyond words,

beyond reason,

beyond anything I've ever known.

He's a gentle reminder that love doesn't have to hurt to be real,

and that God still writes love stories in His own time.

A perfect kind of love,

from an imperfect man,

that fits my life so perfectly,

it feels like grace.

Yeah... he's different.

I Got You

I need you to know that,

No matter what,

I got you.

This world can be a bitch,

Especially to the best, and

Life is at fault too.

You try to do right,

Give it your all, but

Life shoots you down

Every time.

You want to give up.

It seems like the easier way out, and

It is but

It is not the right way, so

You don't give up—

Down but never out.

Like you have a racket in your hand,

Throwing back everything life throws at you.

NATALYA

I see you, King.

And although you are standing tall and

Getting through life's hurdles,

You're still amazing.

Just know

I am here if you need me,

To have and to hold

You down for whatever

Whenever

Forever.

I love you

And

I need you.

My being needs yours.

My lungs need the same air you breathe

So I can be close to you,

To smell you.

Almost like I can touch you with my life.

Your soul makes me smile.

You lack nothing.

I love it here.

I got you.

King

Your antics make me smile.

A simple *"You busy?"* makes my entire day.

You have changed my world

For the better,

Through the worse.

Changing rules and beliefs,

Trying to make sense of it all.

It doesn't—

But at the same time, it does.

There's no way you aren't for me.

A real King

That matches me to a T.

HNIC and HBIC—

It takes one to know the other.

That's us.

Like Bey said, *"I see your hustle with my hustle, I can keep you,"*

And I can.

I bring a whole table and

I'll place it next to yours.

You're still seated at the head as

A real King

That matches me to a T.

I'll be your Queen.

I got your back,

And I know you have mine.

Nothing can stop us but us.

Let me cater to you, King.

I see you.

I respect you.

You deserve nothing less than the best.

Something different.

Behind a towel and a wall

Is me,

A Queen fit for A King.

Only Me

I wish someone was here.

Not for sex but

To hold me.

To make me feel that

Everything is good.

Life is good and

Goes on.

The bullshit he pulled should be unforgiven, but forgiveness is
for me so

I forgive you—but

Never again

Will I play the fool.

I believed you when you said you loved me, but

In that same year, you were trying to love

Someone else.

You had future plans for them and

You.

Not me.

Every part of me wants to regret,

But I won't.

Everything I went through

Is bringing me to whoever God has for me, and

He will respect and value me.

No, he won't be perfect, but

He'll be perfect for me.

He won't have to lie

Cheat

Deceit or

Cause anyone pain or

Heartbreak.

The love will be real and

Sincere.

God will send me my person,

The one who I should've waited for

From the beginning.

Every part of me wants to regret,

But I won't.

Like every great artist,

I must fall so my come-up

NATALYA

Will be just as grand.

I still wish someone was here

To hold me and tell me

Everything is going to be ok.

Interrupted

How did we get here?

How could I let this happen?

Heartbroken?

Again?

My heart doesn't know any better,

But I do.

My heart doesn't want to accept it.

I don't either.

How can I be heartbroken by someone I've never had?

Even though it wasn't physical,

I've had him;

We've had each other.

We fucked our brains out.

I mean our minds.

We know each other deep within.

Our likes.

Our dislikes.

Our childhoods.

NATALYA

Our fantasies.

Or how we tease.

I fell in love with him.

He fell in love with me.

Nothing else mattered,

Especially time.

¡Tenemos nuestro mundo!

Nothing can stop this.

I love him enough to leave him alone,

But his conflict played a part.

I love him enough to let him go,

Because rule number one is

Never be number two.

I love him enough to not care—but

I ... We interrupted his life.

I've had him without having him.

My soul craves him and

My body does too.

Now I'm conflicted.

I respect him enough to let him go but—

I don't want to.

I'm heartbroken

Again.

Love Again

One day ... the pain will let go.

The tears will dry.

This heart—

this broken, bleeding, beautiful heart—

will heal.

And I will no longer cry.

The sunshine will cut through the storm,

light breaking across my scars,

and I'll stand ready,

open-handed,

to give love another try.

But listen—

this time will be different.

This time I will not hand over all of me too soon.

This time, I will guard the fire inside my chest.

Because not everyone,

NOT everyone,

is built to hold the heat of a woman like me.

See, I love in electric hues.

I pour like rivers.

And some men—

they only come with paper cups.

They can't hold it.

They can't taste it.

They spill what they don't understand.

But I know ... God has someone.

Someone with hands strong enough,

a spirit patient enough,

a heart open wide enough

to receive me.

I don't know why the last one had to end—

why betrayal dressed itself in love,

why lies wore the mask of forever.

But I've learned

when love blinds you,

you stop seeing clearly,

you confuse chains for closeness,

you mistake silence for peace.

NATALYA

So, until then ...

until God sends the one carved for me,

I will gather the pieces of my heart,

not ashamed of the cracks,

not ashamed of the breaks.

Because next time, I'll take it easy.

Next time, I'll take it slow.

'Cause real love cannot—

no,

real love should not

be rushed.

New Shirt

You see a nice shirt.

You like it.

It's beautiful;

It's new.

So, you get it.

You buy pretty accessories that go perfect with it.

You wear it.

You show it off.

You're loving the attention.

You love how you feel.

It's your favorite shirt.

But as the days, weeks, months, years—maybe not that long—

But as time goes by

You lose interest.

You're ready for a new shirt,

A different one.

You want that feeling again,

The one a new shirt gives you.

NATALYA

So, you go out in search of a new shirt.

You find it,

Or it finds you.

You like it.

It's beautiful;

It's new.

You get it.

Your once favorite shirt

Is now old to you.

It takes its place in the back of your closet—no,

Your drawer,

And you introduce your new shirt to your world.

You show it off.

You're loving the attention.

You love how you feel again.

But it seems not to fit you;

You adjust yourself

And it does.

It fits perfectly.

Through It All

When life happens, it seems it takes a turn for the worst.

At times, it even seems like you can drown in a glass of water.

Know that God is there willing to help you through the storm,

Through the trials,

Through the pain.

Seems easier said than done?

Maybe, but,

Try Him.

Talk to Him.

Open your heart to receive what He has for you.

Open your mind.

Just make sure to have the understanding that,

Most likely,

It may not be what you want to hear,

But—

It will be EXACTLY what you need to walk on water and ...

Dance in the rain.

For My Daughter and Her Wife

In life, none of us truly know what we are dealt. Life can feel normal to us and yet completely abnormal to others. But, in the end, the result can be as beautiful as two people who love each other no matter what.

As a mom, it was hard, but as a human, it was easy—knowing that my daughter has found someone who makes her happy. And that's what it's all about. Both of you have endured the test of life, the test of time, the test of gossip, and the test of everything that was supposed to be wrong—and yet you made it right. You love each other beyond measure, beyond words, beyond society, beyond what is deemed correct or incorrect. For that, I love you both dearly and hold you close to my heart.

What you have endured has only tested your love, showing that together, you can survive anything life throws your way. Life will play its crazy games, and things might seem to fall apart at the first sign of turmoil, but you two have proof: *together, love can survive anything*. I love you both to life, and I pray that people see the beauty and strength of your love—through every hurdle, through every hurt, through every doubt, through it all. Love always wins.

For My Son and His Wife

I pray you never forget this moment—this feeling right here. Remember who you were in your single days, who you are becoming in your married days, and who you will be in your parenting days. Life will come with its twists and turns, its storms and its sunshine, but when it does, remember this moment—when your love reached beyond words, beyond days, beyond kids, beyond life itself.

Let that love carry you through whatever life throws your way. As humans, we will go through things, but it is your love for each other that will endure. You have taken the time to truly know each other before saying "I do," and that is the foundation of something lasting.

Don't let Instagram reels, TikTok trends, or Facebook posts define what love looks like. Don't let other people's pain become your pattern. No other man, no other woman, can come close to what the two of you have together. I love you both to life, and I pray your love remains eternal.

You'll Never Meet Another Me

She may be prettier,

her face soft, her smile bright.

She may be younger,

with smooth skin and wide-eyed wonder.

But she will never be me.

She won't know your secrets

before you whisper them.

She won't catch the shift in your tone,

read the storms in your silence,

or know the weight behind your laughter.

She won't have scars

that mirror the ones you hide,

won't carry the fire

that matches your wild.

She may dress it up,

make you feel like you've won—

but she will never taste like history.

Never love you in a language

you didn't know you spoke.

Never touch your soul

and set it ablaze.

You'll learn, in time,

what I already know—

women are everywhere,

but a force like me?

Not many.

You will only get to experience me

once in a lifetime.

Something New

It's over.

My mind is clouded, and questions arise.

What happened?

I thought love stood the test of time.

A mix of emotions take over my heart, and

I'm doubting myself and who I am.

Am I good enough?

What could I have done better?

But then as I stop and begin rebuilding myself and clearing my head,

I realize there was nothing more to do.

I just wasn't their person.

Then one day it happens.

Someone new came into my life

And woke up the beautiful woman inside of me

Like Deborah Cox, I asked how the hell did you get here?

Where did you come from?

I never thought someone could ever make me feel optimistic for love again.

I am not confused but intrigued yet nervous.

I'm not scared.

I'm not in a rush.

This is different.

I'm not a kid; I know better.

Good things come to those who wait.

Right?

This feels right.

THE BAD

Raw confessions of a woman at her breaking point. After a decade of sacrifice and empty promises, she faces the truth that love without intimacy is no love at all. "The Bad" are pieces that confront grief, betrayal, loss, loneliness, and the ache of letting go.

Bad At Love

You love love,

but you're fucking bad at it.

You love the idea of love—

the chase, the thrill,

the soft lips,

the easy lies.

You love love,

but you're fucking bad at it.

Can't escape

your fucking bad habits.

Really fucking bad at it—

pouring poison into your own glass.

Same patterns,

same bullshit,

different faces.

Feeding your ego,

stroking the surface,

while your soul starves.

NATALYA

You love love,

but you're fucking bad at it.

Had too many simple bitches,

now you don't even know

what real love is anymore.

You call it freedom;

I call it fear.

You call it fun;

I call it lonely.

And every time real love

knocks at your door,

you slam it shut—

because it asks for honesty,

for patience,

for growth you aren't ready for.

So, you keep fucking up

a real love,

trading diamonds for dirt,

trading substance for smoke.

You're not heartless;

you're just reckless.

Not broken

but afraid to be whole.

You love love,

but your fucking bad at it.

You just can't escape all your fucking bad habits.

You had way too many simple bitches,

and you don't know what real love is anymore.

You keep fucking up a real one.

And that's the worst kind of bad—

wanting love so bad

you burn it down

before it can even fucking really get started.

Priceless

Your love is different now.

That fiery feeling you used to get when you thought of me has faded.

Your *I love yous* come out sounding forced, sometimes not at all.

I want to say I don't know what happened, but I'd be lying—because I do. The change happened when I created boundaries.

Your actions started to interfere with my peace, and I can't have that. The peace I have now came at a price—random crying, sleepless nights. Yeah, expensive as hell.

That shouldn't have been the reason you changed. Maybe you fell out of love with me, but the timeline doesn't match. Our bond was too strong for that.

You asked me, "If you're not happy, why not just call it quits?"

The truth is, I am happy with you. I'm just not happy with what you do. But that's not enough reason for me to let go—because if you met me halfway, we could fix this.

But you don't want to.

So, it's clear to me—you're done.

The change happened when I created boundaries.

I still love you ... but I love me, too.

Heartbroken

If there was such a thing as perfect,

you would come closer than any man ever.

The way you love me,

the way you make me feel like the only woman in the world.

Strong in your presence,

confident in who you are—

provider,

protector,

a man I could lean on.

Not without flaws,

but then, none of us are.

Even your battles with the bottle—

I can look past that.

But what I cannot get over

are the empty nights,

the silence of waiting,

the ache of you returning days later

as if my tears never fell

and my heartbreak didn't matter.

The nights you don't come home,

the mornings I wake up alone,

or you return like nothing happened.

That is the wound I cannot carry.

That is the line I cannot cross.

I love you with everything in me,

and it breaks me to say it.

But—

I can't do this anymore.

Foolish

How did I get myself into this?

Having someone for me

Is absolutely something that I want;

However,

He wasn't free to love.

I should've just kept my hot tail quiet.

Not pursue

Not engage

Not flirt

Not get to know him—

Especially not fall in love.

And now I'm heartbroken.

Not because I don't have him, because I do.

Not because he doesn't love me, because he does.

At least he says he does,

And he shows me that he does.

I'm still heartbroken because he's not mine.

Although he is—

NATALYA

Not technically.

Foolish.

Yeah, that's it.

But am I?

Maybe in thinking that someone would choose me for a change.

Maybe in thinking that I could be the one

For him.

Foolish.

Yes, that's it.

No matter how it's defined,

Here I am all alone.

I'm not privy to the time I want

And only privy

To the time I get.

Spare time.

Whatever is left over.

Foolish.

Yeah, that's it.

I must become (un)foolish, but it comes with self-love.

To love myself enough to choose me

And enough to make sure others choose me first.

Otherwise,

Foolish.

Yeah, that's it.

Nothing's going to change

If I don't change,

If I don't require respect.

Respect.

Yeah, that's it.

As pretty as I want to paint this picture

And as pretty as this picture looks,

Truth is, it's not real.

Oh, my pretty self is his

For sure.

We made sure of that,

But

He's not mine;

He's not with me.

I'm settling for borrowed time,

More like sometimes.

NATALYA

And that's what makes me foolish.

Yeah, that's it.

Foolish.

Say It

Why can't men …

I mean

Why can't people just be straight the fuck up?!

Women aren't …

I mean

People aren't mind readers.

The fuck!

What do you want?

No no, what the fuck do you really want?

Or do you even know?

A fuck buddy?

A real woman …

I mean

A forever partner?

Or just someone to play with?

Regardless of your reason

Just fuckin' say it.

Say what the fuck you want!

NATALYA

I'm not …

I mean

People are not mind readers.

Men …

I mean

People reach out to the public for answers.

The ones who entertain their ego.

Yeah, I'm talking about that Fakebook.

Why?

Be a man.

A grown up.

Besides, you should …

I mean

People should already have the answers they seek.

Just be the fuck honest with yourself that

You weren't ready for someone like me,

Who loves flaws and all

And

Doesn't want anything from you but love.

And you …

I mean

People need to be real with the one they allegedly want.

Just make sure you're ready for what the fuck you want.

Or is it that you miss that past life?

The one you wanted to escape from.

I don't have time …

I mean

People don't have time for the bullshit.

I mean

Games.

Nah, fuck that,

I meant bullshit.

Just fucking say it.

What the fuck do you want?

No Victims Here

I'm upset with you—

No, more like hurt.

I try to stay away,

But my mind won't let me.

I fucking miss you,

And I hate it.

When you said,

"I hate that I love that I hate that I love you!"

I felt that.

That's why I said, *"Same."*

No victims here.

We both held the knife.

But still—

It sucks.

Your silence,

Your distance,

The way your actions say

You don't give a damn about how I feel—

That's the part that cuts the deepest.

And even now,

Knowing all this,

I still miss you.

And I hate that I still care.

But I do.

You Were Gone Before You Left

Go live your happily ever after.

Doesn't seem like I'm part of it.

Your mouth says one thing—

and when we're together,

your actions echo the lie so well.

But it's on the days

when you don't give a fuck

about how I feel—

those are the days

I finally believe

you never did.

It's the silence that screams now.

The delay in your responses.

The absence in your presence.

You hold me like you still want me

but leave me like you never did.

I told myself to be patient.

Told myself love takes time.

Told myself I was worth the wait—

but you never stopped making me wait.

And now ... I don't feel much of anything.

No anger.

No hope.

Just stillness.

You thought you had me blind,

but I saw it all.

I just chose not to speak.

I played the fool

to fool the fool

who thought he was fooling me.

Grace Under Fire

The fiercest fire burns slow—

from a heart too good to break.

They hold their anger like a secret,

a quiet storm beneath calm waters.

They forgive.

They stay patient.

They bend without breaking,

because grace is their armor.

But every spirit has a limit,

a sacred line divinely drawn.

When that line is crossed,

it's not just anger—it's justice,

a righteous roar sent from above.

The most dangerous anger

is born from mercy worn thin,

from love stretched to its edges,

and a soul ready to protect what God entrusted.

Don't mistake their calm

for weakness or surrender.

Don't push a good heart too far—

or you'll meet a storm

you never saw coming.

Like a Clown

Like a clown,

I wear high spirits—

making others laugh,

so they don't see

the pain deep inside my soul.

Like a clown,

I hide my true feelings,

how hurt I truly am

when the one I love—

my love—

is no longer in love with me.

Like a clown,

I put on my big girl shoes

and walk with head held high,

knowing I gave it my all,

and it still wasn't enough.

Like a clown,

I wear my smile—

but don't mistake it for weakness.

Behind this mask,

there's a heart ready to rise,

and a soul that won't be fooled again.

The Fuck Just Happened?

One minute,

we're good—

in love,

on top of the world.

Untouchable.

Unstoppable.

I thought we finally won.

Now you're gone.

Saying you need time,

time to think.

Telling me life is too heavy,

that you're not okay.

But aren't we supposed to be a team?

Your pain is my pain;

your fight is my fight.

I chose you—

not just the joy,

but the weight too.

Talk to me.

Let me in.

Let me carry some of this with you.

Because right now,

I don't just feel left behind—

I feel ghosted.

Abandoned.

And that's the part that burns.

Because we were supposed to be partners.

Your storm is my storm.

Your war is my war.

You don't get to vanish

and leave me holding "us" by myself.

So, tell me.

Are we on the same team,

or am I just a placeholder

you walk away from

when life gets rough?

Glass Houses

When I came to you,

no judgment—none.

I didn't need your past,

only what you told me,

That was enough.

You were honest with me, or so I thought.

Never asked questions just to judge,

and that's what I loved—

because we both lived in glass houses,

and who's without sin to throw the first stone?

Right?

But this ...

Yes, my baby did this.

Even after I found out she bribed you,

You let it happen.

That cuts deep.

You can think what you want,

but it hurts.

I want this over.

I'm trying to move on.

But she's in my face every day,

and I see her,

knowing she's been under you,

on top of you,

riding the dick that's mine.

That shit burns me to my core.

Whether it was a month, two days, two minutes—

I don't care.

You want to downplay it?

That's the truth.

Yea, my baby did that.

If that was your past,

and you were young—fine.

But you're older now,

married.

Is this hard to swallow?

Fuck yes.

Everything in me wants to run—

NATALYA

but my feet won't move.

They just won't.

92

The Choice Was Yours

I'm not trying to argue, baby.

I just need to respond to something you said.

I never accused y'all of anything—

and definitely not for two years.

What I did say, over and over,

was that I could feel she liked you.

You even admitted that she liked to watch you, remember?

She confirmed that much herself.

I told you that.

But I didn't accuse you of crossing any lines.

Not until you started staying out all night,

claiming it was work.

But the money wasn't matching the hours.

That's when I started getting suspicious.

I saw things I didn't want to believe.

And, even then, I refused to believe my man

would stoop so low,

especially not with some little girl.

NATALYA

Like I've said before,

I'm grown—

and I am not responsible for your choices.

But so are you.

Being a man means knowing better.

You should've stayed away.

Uninvited

Why can't I be a part of your world?

You always leave me behind

to be with your close friends—

the ones tied to a version of you I've never met,

a life I was never part of.

They know the inside jokes.

They remember when.

They get to see you relaxed, unguarded—

and I'm left on the outside,

wondering when I'll be let in.

You say I'm important.

You say it's nothing.

But nothing shouldn't feel like this—

a locked door

with your laughter echoing behind it.

There's something,

or someone,

you still carry

in the rooms you won't let me in.

Why am I always the one left waiting

while you return to the parts of yourself

I've never been invited to?

Why does yesterday get more of you

than I do?

The Woman in the Mirror

I poured into him.

Not just love,

but time, sacrifice,

quiet prayers whispered while he slept.

I made meals from nothing

and turned them into comfort.

Rubbed his back when stress bent him

like a tired tree in the wind.

I held his dreams like sacred things—

woke up early so he could sleep in,

stood behind him while he tried

to build something for us.

It was never just about me.

I made sure of that.

I was his peace,

his plan B,

his unpaid therapist,

his silent strength.

NATALYA

The kind of woman who shows up

even when she's exhausted,

even when she's breaking.

And what did he do with all I gave?

He gave his body to someone else.

His time.

His stories.

Maybe even pieces of his laughter

—the same ones that used to belong to me.

He didn't tell me.

I found out.

Quietly.

Painfully.

One misplaced text,

one unfamiliar name that suddenly

felt like it had lived in our home

longer than I had.

I stood in the mirror

and asked myself the questions

no woman wants to ask:

Was I not enough?

Was I too much?

Did he ever even see me—really see me?

He said it was a mistake.

That it "meant nothing."

Funny how something that meant nothing

could shatter everything.

I bent.

But I didn't break.

I gathered the pieces.

Not with drama.

Not with revenge.

Just with the quiet power

of someone who finally remembered

what she was worth.

I left.

Yeah, I cried.

But then ...

I rose.

Gathered every piece of me he tried to forge.

NATALYA

No scene.

No slam of the door.

No malice.

Just that quiet, solid kind of power

that says:

I remember who I am.

Disappointed

"For better or for worse ... Through sickness and in health ... Till death do us part,"

Is what you said,

But it seems like you've abandoned me

When I need you the most.

I took those same vows

On that same day,

And I have never given up on you.

I've stopped doing for me

To do for you,

For Us,

And you treat me like I'm the worst person

In your world.

I am hurt—

More like disappointed.

No, fuck that.

I'm both

Hurt AND disappointed.

All I keep thinking is

NATALYA

I wouldn't do that to you.

No, fuck that.

I've never done that to you.

But you've never done that to me.

What I loved the most about us is

"I eat, we eat."

But now I feel like you would let me starve

For help

For attention

For you.

I am hurt—

More like disappointed.

No, fuck that.

I'm both

Hurt AND disappointed.

I refuse to believe that

You threw it all away ... for what?

A child

One you saw before she became of age.

A child

One who just turned of age.

A child

Someone who doesn't have shit to offer you

But has you open like this.

A child

Your brother's child.

Made you lose your friend

And has made you want to lose your wife.

I am hurt—

More like disappointed.

No, fuck that.

I'm both

Hurt AND disappointed.

That's fucked up.

Her

She's not me.

She could never be me.

The woman I am,

the wife I was,

the person you once swore you loved.

She's not me.

She could never be me.

The fantasy that lingers,

the spark that blows you mind—

beyond words, beyond reason.

She's not me.

She could never be me.

The one in your corner,

the one that has your back

even when you couldn't find your own strength.

She's not me.

She could never be me.

The one who makes love to your mind

and fucks you with no rules

in the very same night.

She's not me.

She could never be me.

The hand that catches your tears

when the weight gets too heavy,

still lifting you high

as the King I see in you.

She's not me.

She could never be me.

But I'm not the one you want.

You want her—

the fleeting rush,

the flame that burns hot then fades,

the high that drops you

the second it's gone.

She's not me.

She could never be me.

I'm the steady fire,

the quiet place where you don't have to be "the man."

NATALYA

With me, you're safe;

with her, you're pretending.

She's not me.

She could never be me.

And now, as the smoke clears

and the thrill of her fades,

you realize

you lost a good thing.

I was the main bitch in your empire,

the legacy we were building,

the forever life we were shaping.

And she?

She was only a moment.

A quick fuck.

A weak high.

A cheap thrill you'll regret

every time you roll over

and feel the empty space

where I used to be.

Because she?

She's nothing.

A shadow you fooled yourself into chasing.

And now you know—

nah, you already knew—

I'm the one you'll never be able to fuckin' replace.

Behind the Door

It's not that I don't care.

I just don't know how to share

the parts of me that have already been seen

by people who knew me

before I knew what I wanted.

You ask to come with me,

to meet the friends who know my history.

But history is heavy,

and some chapters still feel

unfinished,

even when I swear they're closed.

It's easier to keep you separate.

Not because you don't belong

but because I'm afraid

of what might surface

if everything collides.

You say I shut you out.

Maybe I do.

Maybe I don't know

how to let you all the way in

without losing the version of me

you've come to love.

There's no lock on the door—

just fear.

And silence.

And a past I still carry

in corners I haven't cleaned out yet.

But I see you waiting.

I hear you knocking.

And I know

if I don't open up soon,

you'll walk away—

not because you stopped caring

but because you finally realized

you were never the one hiding.

I was.

We're Not Each Other's Priority Anymore

When you say your "I do's,"

you're promising to make each other

your top priority—

above anything and anyone else.

But when that essential part

gets lost in the shuffle,

you risk losing the person

who once meant the world to you.

If you're no longer making your husband

a priority in your life—

or he's not making you his—

it's going to be really hard

to stay a solid unit.

Try going back to prioritizing

your time together,

each other's feelings,

and each other's goals—

to find your way back

to a healthy place

before it's too late.

Can't remember your last date night?

If you're not planning special moments,

and not spending time together,

that's not good news for your relationship.

Make an effort.

Get a couple outings on the calendar,

maybe a movie night

or dinner at your favorite spot,

and see if you can rekindle the flame.

Marriage takes work,

and putting effort into the things

that bond you as a couple

is part of that work.

FUCK IT ALL

Fuck you.

Fuck you.

And most of all—

Fuck you.

I'm done.

I'm done with everyone.

Everything.

Every fake promise, every half-assed excuse.

Fuck you.

I'm so fucking tired.

Tired of loving you harder than you ever deserved.

Tired of twisting myself into knots

Just to make you feel whole

While I bled out for you.

Yup. Fool.

That's me—

The crowned queen of pretending.

Give me the gotdamn Emmy.

The Oscar.

All of it.

I earned it, didn't I?

I made you believe your own lies.

I let you think you were worth my truth.

I let myself believe you'd love me enough—

Enough to stay loyal,

Enough to show up unconditional,

Enough to make me feel like I wasn't screaming into a void.

Fuck you.

Fuck every *I love you* you spat out like stale gum.

Fuck every fake future you painted on my walls

And left to peel.

Fuck you

For taking my heart,

For opening my love,

And leaving me empty-handed.

But here's the twist:

You don't get to keep my anger.

You don't get to feed on my rage.

NATALYA

You don't get to wear my name like a stain.

I'll take my love back—

Every piece you thought you owned.

I'll leave you standing in your ruins,

Naked, exposed, choking on your own bullshit.

And when you reach out, crying for me to come back,

You'll find nothing but my silence.

Remember her?

Remember that scene when a husband had it all and a good wife and one day he put her out of his life and let someone else in and then tragedy struck him and the new someone kicked him while he was down taking everything and his wife came back picked him up off the ground and brought him back to his feet and then blessed him with a kiss and left and he was hurt because he lost a good woman? Didn't just happen in a movie.

Karma.

Nope

Let me stop right there.

I get it.

A man will do for who he wants, and

A man will love who he wants.

And me?

I was just a lesson that hopefully you learned

Unconditional love is really a thing.

But—seems I didn't live up to your expectations.

Turns out, none of it mattered.

Being a good woman.

Being there for you.

Being everything you needed.

All of it—worthless

in your rules of love.

So, I step back.

I play my new position now.

Praying for strength—

because loving you like I did,

giving all of me,

and getting nothing in return?

That's a war.

And I fought it alone.

I'll never love anyone else the way I loved you.

Because love this deep,

and getting nothing back,

was a waste of my fire.

Whoever said,

It's better to have loved and lost than never to have loved at all

clearly never got burned the way I did.

Honestly?

I'd rather never have loved at all.

But don't get it twisted—

I'm broken but not shattered.

I'm still fire.

I'm still a storm.

I'm still me,

while you're still lost,

trying to figure out what the fuck it is you want.

Done

I can't take this no-love thing any longer.

I've tried—God knows I've tried—

but I'm done begging for scraps.

I want love,

not just your busy hands counting dollars

while I sit here starving for touch.

A gift card gathering dust,

a bank account fat and silent.

We don't even spend it on each other.

Not a dinner, not a movie, not a moment.

So many years of fires and ashes,

and somehow we rose, still together,

but for what?

To be ghosts in the same house?

To watch the clock bleed our youth away?

You once said money makes your dick hard—

your words, not mine.

So, I broke my back to build my own empire

after helping you build yours,

thinking maybe I'd earn your gaze,

your hand on my back,

your mouth on my name.

I got the money—but you?

You're physically here with me,

but your attention is somewhere else.

I can't take this no-love thing any longer.

I won't.

A marriage isn't supposed to rot

just because we're busy.

We chose to let it rot.

Do you remember your promises?

Keep my money; I'll handle everything.

Stay, you said.

So, I stayed. Like a fool.

But I hear your stories.

I see your hints.

I'm not deaf. I'm not blind.

And I'm done pretending.

NATALYA

So, this is me leaving.

Keep the gift card. Keep the bank.

Keep your hard dick and your soft lies.

I'm taking my love—

the real currency—

and spending it somewhere else.

Where it's wanted.

Life Is Too Short

I've learned, in losing those I love,

how fragile breath is—

how swift the shadows fall.

We don't know the hour,

the day, the moment

when goodbye comes sudden and silent.

So, say I love you often.

Let those words be the light

filling every space in between,

your voice brushing skin like a secret touch—

soft, urgent, real.

Make peace within yourself

and with the ones who walk beside you.

The way you hold them now

will echo in your heart

the day they slip away,

when silence screams

what was never said.

NATALYA

No room for shoulda, coulda, woulda—

only the weight of this moment,

heavy with raw, trembling love.

You will still ache,

still miss the warmth that's gone.

But your soul will settle,

wrapped in the softness of truth given freely—

a quiet peace,

a balm for the heart,

a gentle promise kept.

Confused

My heart is sad and so confused.

I'm praying for clarity.

Some light in this dark time.

I am full of love and thought that it would be ok to

Give it all to you, but

You don't feel the same about love.

And that's ok.

Well,

It's going to have to be.

I'm going to have to be ok with that.

I'm not mad.

I respect your honesty.

I just have to shift myself

From what I thought.

From girlfriend

From wifey

From soulmate.

To companion

NATALYA

To roommate

To a forever buddy.

I'm just asking you to bear with me

While I shift.

I won't lie.

It won't be easy.

You'll probably giggle and do your *"okay lol"* thing, but I'm serious.

I'm sorry I misread it.

I misread you.

I misread us.

My heart is sad and so confused.

The times we talked

The intimacy we shared

The nights we bonded

Seemingly were only good for that time.

That place

That season.

Like that song says

"I can't make you love me."

And I didn't try to make you.

Yet you did.

What happened?

My heart is sad and so confused.

Although I noticed

I should have known.

You don't initiate I love yous anymore.

You respond to mine,

A kind of response.

Ewww.

Although I noticed

I should have known.

You don't crave me anymore.

Not just sexually.

The type of crave that would make my day

Just from seeing your good morning texts.

That crave.

I need you to be honest with me,

With yourself.

Oh, wait.

You were.

You want a companion

A roommate

A forever buddy.

So do I, but

I want love too.

My heart is sad and so confused.

Something Borrowed

"That's exactly what I wanted," said no one ever

Regarding something borrowed.

That is NOT the goal.

Something new

that I can call my own,

I can love on and

make mine

and to have and to hold.

And it's mine.

It may have some bumps and bruises from its travels.

Even something new is not perfect.

Something old we cherish.

In many ways, it's new to you.

It holds value in your heart and is worth loving on some more.

Something blue may have been damaged a little bit in transition, but

with tender love and care,

together

we can look forward to better days.

NATALYA

Not perfection.

Just perfect for me,

for us.

Something borrowed is wrong,

especially when you fall in love.

And

then you have to return it.

But

You don't want to.

But you should.

And you have to.

But I want it for me.

I want it in my life.

It completes me.

It makes me feel like nothing or no one

ever.

And maybe nothing or no one ever will.

But

it shouldn't have been borrowed in the first place.

Something so valuable

that wasn't given to you.

Because

it holds a lot of value in someone else's heart.

Who am I to rip it apart

from their grasp?

Out of the depth of someone's being ...

Something borrowed without knowledge is just as good as stolen.

But you don't want to let it go.

This Is Crazy

This is crazy

how I feel about someone I never had.

But I have.

I've had his mind.

I fell for it—

the way he talked,

his kiss.

How can I feel a way about him being there

and not here

with me?

This is crazy.

What does she have that I don't?

Him.

She has him.

My whole heart wants to think he is being held

against his will.

But he's not.

That's his house.

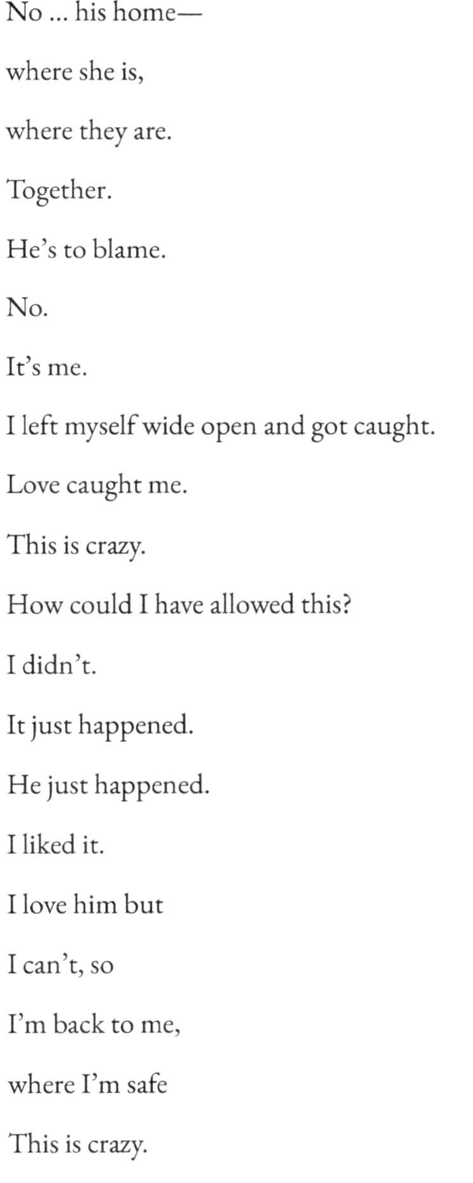

No ... his home—

where she is,

where they are.

Together.

He's to blame.

No.

It's me.

I left myself wide open and got caught.

Love caught me.

This is crazy.

How could I have allowed this?

I didn't.

It just happened.

He just happened.

I liked it.

I love him but

I can't, so

I'm back to me,

where I'm safe

This is crazy.

Caught

I opened the door.

And there you were.

With …

Her.

In our bed.

Hands where mine should be.

Lips pressing promises you once whispered to me.

I froze.

Time slowed.

Years of love, trust, and everything we built—

shattered in one heartbeat.

You didn't see me.

Or maybe you did.

And didn't care.

I wanted to scream.

To break, to burn, to tear.

I wanted revenge.

But instead, I watched.

Saw everything.

Felt everything.

The lies,

the I love yous,

the promises whispered to me—

all meant for her.

I should have broken.

I should have fallen.

But I didn't.

I am not a fool.

I am not a victim.

I am the woman

you could not keep.

So, take her.

Take your betrayal.

Take your shame.

I am walking out.

With my dignity.

Classy.

With the love that is still mine—

and ready to give to someone who deserves it.

And you?

You'll remember me.

Not for what you stole

but for what you lost.

Reclaim

I played the fool.

Too long.

You lied.

All along.

In your truck.

In our bed.

I have proof.

No excuses.

No hiding.

I see the truth.

Every lie.

Every move.

Step aside?

Ok, excuse me.

She's your #1—for now.

Until you're done.

Until someone else fits your game.

I found my place.

NATALYA

I raised our babies.

I helped your family.

My work here is done.

This season is mine.

Self-love.

Respect.

Reclaim.

You said love was gone.

You wanted a business partner.

Fine.

But my love?

Not for you.

Never again.

Beyoncé said it best.

"It's not the cheating that hurts;

it's the type of bitch you cheat with."

But

Is it the mistake that hurts, or

Is it the girl you chose instead of me?

My mistake was

Always being about you.

Too many years of this shit.

Not anymore:

I rise.

I leave.

I take my love.

My fire.

My life.

Chapter One: Me

I hear you—I truly do.

But I refuse to accept this *"take it or leave it"* stance,

like I'm just something to discard.

If you truly cared, you'd stand and say she's wrong.

You'd fix what's broken, no matter the cost.

Because if the roles were reversed,

if the locks were tampered with on your door,

there'd be no silence, no ignoring—

only storms and consequences.

Yet here I stand, still understanding, still trying to believe.

I think about us, about everything we built.

And I wonder—why not simply say the truth?

If your heart no longer belongs here,

why not just tell me?

You push me away,

making me feel the blame is mine.

And your words are sharper than knives—

quiet cuts that bleed deep.

To let someone fall so hard,

then pick apart every flaw

as if it justifies the hurt,

to seek another and leave me standing,

carrying the weight of your fault—alone.

How it felt to hear you say,

Did you think this would last?

I'm not the lovey type.

Or worse—

I don't want to be close anymore.

And what of me?

You are all I have,

but do you care for my heart?

Or the damage done,

the marriage unraveling?

Sometimes I wonder if you're the one

who can't

or won't – let go.

You are the one who opened the door

to her world, who allows disrespect

NATALYA

to sleep in our home.

I love more deeply, care more fiercely—

and still, I remain,

ready to forgive, to forget,

but it means nothing to you.

So, hear me now. If you're done,

set me free.

Yes, it will hurt

but less than living with someone

who no longer wants me—

who won't walk with me to the corner store

but gives her the world without hesitation.

You told me once,

You must put yourself first.

That was my mistake.

I put you first—

my love, my husband, my provider.

I should have put me first.

I thought it to be selfish,

but it's not.

Now, this next chapter is mine.

I will find love again—

unhindered, unstoppable.

My heart will be his to cherish,

and I will be his, fully and freely.

Remembering not to forget me—

I'm first.

THE NAUGHTY

A raw, erotic snapshot of passion, "The Naughty" are bold, sensual, unapologetic verses exploring longing, lust, secrets, and wild freedom.

Rose

I take you in my hand,

Soft, slick, ready,

Press you hard—right against my clit,

Buzzing, pulsing, insistent,

Driving me wild.

I grind you slow,

Drag every vibration through my slick heat,

Press, push,

Circle,

Press again,

Every stroke lighting fire through me.

I bite my lip,

Arch,

Shiver,

Curl my toes, clench my thighs,

Let the buzz crawl deep.

Make me gasp,

Make me drip,

NATALYA

Make

Me

Moan with every press

Of my PPP,

Pussy Pressure Point.

You hum against me,

Pull every shiver, every quiver, every wet gasp.

I can't stop,

Won't stop,

Lose myself in you, in this filthy pulse.

Every press, every slick hum,

Every teasing grind,

Fucks me over,

Makes me ache, makes me melt,

Until I'm trembling, soaked, gasping—

And I love it.

Love every filthy, needy, desperate second.

Fuck you, Rose.

Crave

It's the good morning text

That's embedded in my mind and

Made its way to my heart.

Who sent you?!

Everything in me wants to say God,

Because

You're what I want

You're what I need

You're what I crave in

My life,

Not just my bed.

Our conversations pierce my soul

My thoughts

My heart.

It's the how you doing texts

That make me smile,

Make my whole day.

As soon as I see it's you,

NATALYA

I feel giddy

Like a school girl seeing her crush.

Nah, it's new but it's familiar, and

It's been a long time

since anyone has had that effect on me.

I miss it.

I want it.

I crave you.

You match everything I am

A hustler

A lover

Everything someone wants and deserves.

Why is life like this?

It's not life.

We're impatient.

In search of the person that completes us,

We test the different flavors like we're at a buffet.

You find something you think you want.

You're full and content

Until you're no longer satisfied with what you had.

It's not what you thought you wanted.

You want that thing you may not be able to have

But it's that thing you still crave.

Like He Missed Me

I come home

He's happy to see me

Like he missed me.

I greet him with a kiss

He hugs me back

Smells my neck

My spot.

Ugh!

He moans in my ear "Mm! You smell good."

My body is burning with desire for him

Now I'm horny.

He walks me back against the arm of the couch

Pulls my skirt up

Grabs a handful of his chocolate dick

And puts it inside me

Slowly but hard

Ugh!

Fuck, he feels amazing!

He's all over me

and and …

… in me

He's fucking me and making love in the same thrust.

Damn, he craves me

His body all over me

My legs up and around his waist

He's holding me by my ass

While his thick finger is in it.

Ugh!

I didn't know that DP would feel that amazing.

He pulls out and I'm squirting

He turns me around

and we start kissing.

That's all me

Take your pussy baby

That's all you.

The heat that flows all through me is inexplicable

My legs tremble

I'm so wet

NATALYA

His dick taking up every inch of my pussy

It's pulsating

He speeds up

I'm cumin

He's cumin

We cum together

Like he missed me.

First Time

Making love for the first time

to the one you love deep in your soul

is a different type of desire.

When he kisses you

like he wants to devour you

and his hand is in your pants

playing with your clit,

you cum ...

instantly.

Hearing him whisper

Baby, I want you

in your ear

while he's kissing

and touching

and grabbing

and biting

and sucking your neck

makes ME want to cum right now.

NATALYA

It's a spontaneous moment

when y'all get in the room.

Clothes coming off,

it's the moment you both have waited for

Anticipated

Desired

Dreamt

of him being inside of you.

You lay on the bed;

he heads straight to the appetizer,

eating that pussy like you're familiar.

Your legs tremble …

Already?!

Thank God you're a woman.

He gets on the bed …

Your turn.

You grab a handful of his dick and

put it in your mouth

and return the favor.

He tastes good,

trying to swallow him like it's your last meal,

so he pushes you because he wants to cum but

inside of you.

You assume the position,

torso flat on the bed,

ass up.

You feel him enter you.

MMMM! Fuck!

Pounding on your shit,

so you throw it back.

Wait …

He turns you around so he doesn't cum yet and

so he can watch you

cum.

He enters you

softly.

You feel him

He feels you

He kisses you

with his tongue

NATALYA

while thrusting

softly

moans in your ear

Baby, I'm inside of you,

while thrusting.

You cum,

pussy throbbing on his dick

sucking it.

He feels you.

He loves it.

He moans.

FUCKKKKK!!

"Yes, baby," you tell him,

"Give it to me!"

He's cumin,

pussy still throbbing on his dick

sucking it.

He lays on you,

dick throbbing

still inside you.

You rub down the sides of his body

slowly

using the tips of your fingers.

They meet middle of his waist.

He jerks.

First time ... amazing.

Detox

My mind is going crazy

Thoughts all over the place—yet

They're stuck on the same thing.

I'm not scared.

Why do we want things we can't have?

Why does that make us want it more?

The same drug that distorts my mind

Is the same drug that relaxes my soul

Dopamine.

I have to detox from this urge

This feeling.

I haven't been this high in years—but

I'm not scared.

I love it.

It loves me.

I need to detox from this craving.

I don't want to interrupt a good thing, because

That life doesn't deserve it

But I deserve it and

It deserves me.

I don't want to come down

From this.

It elevated fast

It's like none ever.

I'm not scared

But I'm scared.

I've never been this high before.

I need to detox

But I don't want to.

Assume the Position

My alarm goes off

I roll my naked body over

I turn that bitch off

My silk sheets slip off my warm body

Exposing my nipples

Ooo ... I'm naked

My body is so warm

A hint of the oil I put on all over me after my shower

Still lingers

So soft

I feel amazing

My pussy is already so wet

I prop my ass up and scooch over to his side

Mmm! I feel that thick dick already ready for me

I feel his arm come around me and grab me

Pulling me closer

I assume the position

Arched back

Easy access

I reach back and grab his dick

I follow the wordless instructions

"Insert here"

Mmm! Si PapÍ!

I assume the position

Leg over his

Pussy exposed

His fingers find my clit

He plays with her at the same rhythm his nature is slipping in

And

Out

In

And

Out of me

I can feel his heartbeat

My pussy is so juicy yet so tight

Sucking every inch he gives me

He loves it

I hear him moan

NATALYA

I love it

He makes me cum

All on it

My muscles tighten around it

Still thrusting

A little faster

He cums

All in me

Our juices mix together

In what seemed like forever

He kisses the back of my neck

We doze off

His alarm goes off

I get a warm wet washcloth

Before I get in the shower

I assume the position

To clean it

Instead, I taste us

I woke up the beast

He grabs my hair

He flips me over

I assume the position

His Side

Woke up, dick hard AS FUCK!

Your ass tooted right up against my dick

Got my mans perfectly seated in your ass crack

HARD as FUCK!

So, I take the tip and place it on that wet pussy—but just the tip tho

Not even to insert it yet

Just letting it slide around as you slowly rock your hips back and forth, trying your damndest to let him slip in …

but I won't let it

I reach around, grabbing and caressing your tits, as I'm slow breathing and kissing on your neck

DAMN!!!!!!

I feel her getting hotter and wetter, altogether …

I take my hand slowly from your breasts, up to your neck, as you tilt that head backwards

Your eyes get thinner, open but closed at the same time

You're biting that bottom lip

I get a better and more firm grip on that neck

My other hand grabs your hip/small of your back

I put him in

She purrs, but not as a cat

She purrs because you can hear how wet she is as I'm throbbing inside of you …

You're moaning

Calling my name

"Give it to me, Papi."

Ugh!

I go deeper

Sliding my dick in and out

Kissing and sucking on your lips

Devouring your soul!

You climb on top of me

Hands placed on my chest

Riding this dick like a rodeo champion

You lean back

My hands are on your breasts

Nipples in my fingertips

I turn you around

Slide back inside of you

NATALYA

Assume the position

The music your ass is making with my thighs sounds like we're clapping in a church choir

"Baby, I'm inside of you."

[Clap Clap Clap Clap]

You throwing it back as I'm beating you forward

Who will budge?

Neither of us

How can we?

We're in sync

You look back at me as if it is time

Time to explode and

Let the floodgates open

Floodgates of your inner being

We have been waiting for this moment

All the talks and all the texts

Composing this very orgasm

We release ourselves, within ourselves

You screaming!

I'm screaming!

"GOT DAMN!!!!!!!!!"

"OH SHIT!!!!!!!!"

We lay there

Together

With smiles but not really smiling

A light that has taken over as if we were Avatars ourselves and have connected the tails

We made it

Babe ... We made it.

Swiss Roll

He dared to taste my passion fruit

without my knowledge.

But I liked that—

how he caught me off guard,

sucked my clit like he was sucking a guinep,

sweet and tart, seed and all.

I wrapped these thick thunder thighs

around his neck,

didn't care if he could breathe or not.

I wanted him drowning in me,

tongue deep in my juice,

his moans humming through my hips.

He tasted the pulp of my hunger,

licked the sugar from the seed,

kept going when my body said stop—

I didn't mean it anyway.

He knew that.

So, I returned the favor,

slid down next to him,

skin still slick, heartbeat still reckless.

On all fours, I started slow—

my taste still fresh on his mouth,

lips sticky with me,

and I sucked it off,

tasting us both at once.

I traced a wet trail down his belly,

tongue teasing the edge of his tattoo,

his hips twitching under my breath.

I licked the crease of his thigh,

felt him throb when I kissed his balls,

my tongue swirling, lazy, hungry.

Then up—

slow drag up his dick,

my lips wrapping 'round the tip,

just the tip—

playful, wicked, soft.

He groaned,

one hand tangled in my hair.

NATALYA

That's when he gave me that cream filling,

sweet, thick, warm on my tongue.

A perfect swirl—

just like a Swiss roll—

rich center hidden inside,

waiting for my bite.

And, baby, I'll keep coming back

for another slice,

another taste,

another roll

'til there's nothing left

but sweet crumbs

and our breath tangled in the dark.

Always on My Mind

As much as I don't want to,

I think about you.

Your existence takes over my thoughts,

and I can't explain it.

Even writing it down,

the words don't come out—

they stay tangled in my chest

where only you can reach them.

Future thoughts of maybe one day

being your wife,

saying I do,

I really do.

Some nights I whisper it to the dark,

testing the weight of your name

next to mine.

I pray it's not me

living a lie,

a soft half-dream I've stitched together

to keep me warm.

I pray it's not just a fantasy—

my fantasy—

but a promise,

waiting for us to be brave enough

to touch it.

Because even when I try to push you out,

you linger—

in my idle thoughts,

in the space beside me when I sleep,

in the secret wish that one day

it'll be your hand I reach for

when I wake up

still wanting.

It's the way you notice things—

the curve of my smile

when I try to hide it,

the way I tuck my hair behind my ear

when I'm nervous,

how you trace the line of my collarbone

like you're reading a secret only you can understand.

It's the way you listen—

not just to my words

but to what I don't say.

Your eyes, steady on mine,

telling me *I see you*.

And that undoing, that quiet surrender—

that's what keeps you lodged in my mind,

woven through my days like soft thread.

Your fingertips remember

the places I forget to love;

your laugh fills the empty corners

where my doubts like to hide.

So, when I pray this isn't just a dream,

what I'm really saying is ...

If I'm dreaming,

don't wake me.

Not yet.

Sexual Frustration

I lay awake, hips heavy with wanting,

tongue pressed to my teeth to hush the curse.

Your back turned, your breath steady, calm—

while I drown in the heat between my own thighs.

I'm here—wet, burning, learning to silence my thighs

so they don't wake the whole house

with how badly they ache for you

to remember they exist.

You forget this body—

the one you once bent over every surface,

the one you moaned into at 2 AM,

the one that still drips when the wind brushes right.

My nipples ache for your teeth,

my neck for your bite,

my hips for your grip—

but you turn over, mouth slack,

dreaming God knows what,

while I grind myself raw against the sheets

like a secret.

Do you know I press my fingers deep,

pretend they're yours?

Pretend you'd wake up and pin me down,

fill me till the only thing I can say is yes, yes, God, yes—

but you don't. You won't.

So, I finish alone, clenching air,

biting my lip so I don't wake you

with the sound of what you're missing.

This bed is big enough for two,

but tonight, it's just me—

wet, angry, alive.

I almost want you to wake up now

and see what you've wasted.

I want you to see me glowing in the dark,

slick with the proof

that I still burn—

with or without you.

As We

As you gaze into my eyes

As your hands sneak between my thighs

As you feel I'm dripping for you

As I feel you're hard, ready to enter my goods

As we can't wait to take it there

As I love it when you pull my hair

As I taste the sweat on your eager skin

As you push inside me, slow then all in

As your fingers dig, teasing, claiming

As my body shivers, craving, naming

As your tongue licks where I burn the most

As I bite my lip, begging you close

As you fuck me hard, pounding deep

As moans escape me, losing sleep

As you grip my hips, pulling me tight

As we move together all through the night

As your breath grows ragged in my ear

As I call your name, loud and clear

As you take me higher, raw and real

As every touch makes me tremble and feel

As we come undone, skin slick and hot

As I ride your wave, giving all I've got

As we collapse tangled, spent and wild

As I know I'm yours—lost in desire

As we take in this moment in time

As we try that position that ends in a 9

As we ...

Marked Territory

I moaned his name once—

soft, breathless,

more like a plea than a sound.

He stopped mid-thrust.

Eyes dark.

Grip firm.

Desire gone feral.

One hand on my throat,

not choking, just claiming—

the other steady at my waist

like he was holding back a storm.

"Say it louder," he commanded,

voice low, dangerous—

the kind of command

you feel in your spine.

He said, *"I want the world to know who owns that pussy."*

So, I said it.

Louder.

With everything he was giving me.

With every filthy stroke

that pushed my insides to the edge.

My back arched,

legs shaking,

nails clawing at sheets like I was losing my mind.

And I swear—

the walls shivered.

My pussy clenched so hard he cursed.

His name shot from my mouth like gospel.

Again. And again.

Until I was nothing but sound and sex and surrender.

And him—

he came with a growl,

buried deep,

like he was marking territory no man would ever touch.

Treading in Dangerous Waters

A mixture of inexplicable emotions leads you to try and maintain composure.

The waters just keep coming in the form of feelings you can't explain and make it hard to stay afloat.

But, for a second, you welcome them.

You feel like you can drown because your body and mind are not where they are supposed to be.

Yet, for a second, you embrace it.

But you can't!

I mean,

you shouldn't 'cause your heart and your body are not free to be there.

It's a scary feeling

It's a new feeling

It's a drowning feeling.

But, for a second,

just for a second,

underneath your—

deep inside your—

Aal the way in your—

you can taste it.

Him.

One Night

I knew what it was

the second you looked at me—

that too-long stare,

that tongue dragging across your bottom lip

like it had already tasted me in your mind.

And maybe I should've walked away.

Maybe I should've pulled my dress down,

held my head up,

acted like a lady raised right.

But I didn't.

Instead, I leaned in,

let your breath tickle my collarbone,

let your hands find the dip in my back

and guide me into a night

I would pretend not to remember

but replay over and over in the shower.

You didn't ask me about my favorite color

or my childhood trauma.

Didn't care what I did for a living.

You just unzipped my dress

like it was a secret

you were aching to tell.

And I let you.

Let your mouth press against skin

that hadn't been kissed in months.

Let your teeth leave little lies

on my thighs and hips.

Let your tongue apologize

for every man who ever left me wanting.

I wasn't thinking about tomorrow—

just the way your hands spread my legs

like pages in a dirty novel.

How you read every moan

like you wrote it.

God, you wrote me.

In grunts and groans,

in bed creaks and headboard taps,

in my own damn name

screamed into your shoulder

as if I was begging to be heard

just one more time.

I won't lie.

I wanted more than just your dick.

I wanted to forget.

To feel something.

To fill the silence that echoes too loud in my bed.

And for a moment—just a night—

you did that.

You silenced it all.

So, no,

I don't regret you.

Not the scratches,

the stains,

the swollen lips,

the way I trembled when you kissed me goodbye.

I regret

how easily I let you in—

not just my body

but the part of me I swore I'd keep locked.

You walked through me

like you had the key

and didn't even know it.

But you'll never know my name,

and I'll never forget your touch.

So, let's call it even.

One night.

No love.

Just truth,

sweat,

and a little bit of sin.

NATALYA

Don't Call This Love

I didn't come for your heart.

I came to ride.

To sweat out frustration,

to fuck the past off my skin

and leave scratch marks on your ego.

You weren't special.

You were available.

And that's all I needed.

I pulled you close,

not to feel safe—

but to feel full.

To remind myself

this body still knows how to take

what it wants.

I said your name

because it was easier than screaming his.

You moaned like you meant it.

Me too.

Your dick was good;

I won't lie.

I bent over the couch,

not for romance,

but because it hit better that way.

I rode you like a problem

I knew how to solve

with no feelings involved.

You touched me like a man

trying to leave an impression.

And, baby, you did—

on my thighs, my neck, my sheets.

But not my soul.

Never that.

So, don't text me good morning.

Don't ask how I slept.

I didn't.

I came, I cleaned up,

and I left your memory on the nightstand

next to my earrings.

NATALYA

Let someone else beg for your time.

I only wanted your body.

And now that I've had it—

I'm good.

All Over Me

I don't just love you—

I crave you.

Like air.

Like water.

Like something my body was never meant to live without.

You're in my mouth

when I try to speak,

in my thoughts

before they even form.

You walk in the room,

and my pulse forgets how to behave.

I want your hands everywhere—

on my skin,

in my hair,

gripping my hips like you're scared I'll vanish.

I don't want space.

I want closeness.

Skin to skin.

NATALYA

Soul to soul.

Obsession wrapped in silk sheets and promises.

You're all over me.

I can't get enough of you

And if this is obsession—

then you're stuck with me

like the scent of you on my skin.

Heat Wave

Your dick is fire,

sliding, pressing, plunging

into every wet, hungry curve,

every part of me that screams for you.

I gasp when your head reaches my sweet spot,

lost in the relentless push of your touch.

At the same time, your mouth and your tongue claiming

and tasting

my lips,

my tongue

You're dragging me higher.

Every thrust, every stroke, every slick press

sends me to a different universe,

making me moan, shiver, shudder—

your body moving with a force I can't resist.

I love it.

I'm raw beneath you,

clinging, begging, screaming

for every inch, every taste, every burn

that only you can deliver.

The heat between us is unbearable,

a storm that crashes, rages, consumes,

leaving nothing but fire, sweat,

and the overwhelming pulse of want.

And when our levees finally break,

I'm dripping, soaked, undone,

already burning for the next surge,

hungry for more of your body,

your mouth, your hands, your fire—

because desire like this

cannot be contained.

No Clothes, No Rules

The world fades the moment the door closes.

No fabric between us, no barriers, no restraint—

just skin, heat, and the ache of wanting.

Your hands roam like they own me,

pressing, stroking, claiming,

every curve, every fold, every shiver

demanding my surrender,

and I give it without hesitation.

I'm submissive.

We tear into each other like fire choking wind,

raw, reckless, and not giving a fuck.

Pleasure thrashes through us in brutal waves,

bodies colliding, dripping, clawing—

breathless curses tangled with moans,

hungry, vicious, insatiably alive.

No words, no pretense, no rules—

just the rhythm of bodies colliding,

the heat of desire unchained,

and the pure, unapologetic ecstasy

of being completely, utterly naked—

in every way.

I arch into you

losing myself in you,

our hearts racing, pulses pounding—

the taste, the touch, the sound of want

mixing in a delicious symphony

that belongs only to this moment,

to us, to this freedom.

And when it ends—if it ever fucking ends—

I'm left dripping, legs shaking,

pussy lubricated and throbbing,

your cum still sliding out of me,

breath ragged, skin burning,

no rules, no mercy—

just your thick dick owning me,

and the hunger that keeps dragging us back for more.

The Art of Temptation

You smile like you know a secret,

devious but sneaky,

and I can't help but lean in—

drawn by the pull of your mischief,

your eyes promising things

that my mind dares not imagine.

Every glance is a challenge,

every word a gentle dare,

your laughter a hook I can't resist,

your touch a whisper along my skin

that leaves me shivering and wanting more.

Flirting is your weapon,

teasing your art,

and I am hopelessly, deliciously caught—

drawn into the rhythm,

the heat, the delicious tension,

unable to escape the gravity of you.

I don't play it cool—fuck that.

NATALYA

The second your hands touch me, I'm soaked,

clit throbbing, pussy begging to be split open.

Your smile isn't charm, it's a command,

a warning that I'm about to be wrecked.

Every brush, every word,

has me dripping down my thighs,

craving your dick fuck me raw,

to pound me until I'm nothing but moans and mess.

I want you to use me,

to break me open on your chocolate rock,

to fuck me past reason, past breath—

until I'm ruined, shaking, dripping,

and still begging for more.

Between the Sheets

The door slams, and the world is gone.

Shadows crawl across the walls,

but I don't see them—only you,

eyes sharp, hungry, devouring,

promising I won't leave this bed the same.

You pull me in hard, deliberate,

fingers dragging fire down my skin.

That shit hurts so fucking good—

teasing, taunting, owning,

making me gasp, making me drip,

my pulse beating like it already belongs to you.

Every movement is an unspoken demand;

your mouth bruises my neck, biting me like saying *Mine*.

My hands claw at you, greedy, wild,

our bodies crashing, grinding, colliding,

exploring every filthy corner of lust—

the familiar twisted darker,

the new pushed deeper, rougher, raw.

NATALYA

Dámelo! I screamed.

Sheets tangle around us like chains;

the bed creaks under the weight of our sin.

Every moan is a confession,

every bite a punishment,

every sexual word another surrender

to the ruin you promise to deliver.

Your touch reminds me

that intimacy can be savage,

that passion can be violent hunger,

and surrender isn't soft; it's brutal,

a giving up of every defense,

a creation of something wicked,

something exquisite,

that can only be born between the sheets.

After the Fight

The anger hasn't left us, thick and sharp in our veins,

but it doesn't matter—because the second our bodies slam together,

there's no room for pride, no room for words.

Only you, only me, only this.

Your hands tear at me, claiming, marking, owning,

letting me know loudly that you're the man.

Tearing my underwear off, you bend me over the couch.

First, your hands, touch my pussy and your finger plunging, curling, dragging fire through every dripping nerve.

Yes! That's what the fuck I want.

I'm so fucking wet, I'm leaking,

pussy quivering around

nothing but hunger—

thick thighs slick, gripping, desperate for your hard dick to bury me deep.

Fuck that, take this dick!

You sit on the chair and my body finds you.

I grind, coil, up and down;

my pussy is sucking your dick.

Your every moan is raw,

shameless,

like a confession of how desperately you want me,

You're begging for more.

I arch my back and you're about to nut.

You push me off

flip me over onto my stomach.

I arch into your favorite angle,

and you slam in, punishing, unrelenting, claiming,

every thrust a mix of obsession, rage, and fire—

your growls dragging me past the edge,

again, and again, until I'm trembling, whimpering,

undone.

Every slam, every gasp, every desperate moan

a reminder that I am yours to destroy,

that I will take it, all of it, endlessly.

Tongue-Tied

You don't ask. You take.

Hands gripping, mouth claiming, teeth grazing.

And I'm already shaking,

both nervous and excited—

kneeling before you like I was made for this.

"Eyes up," you growl, and I obey,

my chest heaving, lips parted, pussy exposed,

aching—

every nerve on fire under your control.

Every touch, every bite, every press

is a command I cannot resist,

a rope tying me tighter to your will.

Your fingers dig, curl, thrust, dragging fire through me,

your voice low, sharp, *"Say it. Tell me who owns this pussy."*

I choke, tongue-tied and desperate.

You smile, cruel and satisfied.

You know exactly how to break me,

how to ruin me,

how to make me beg.

Before I even understand what I'm giving,

I'm under your control.

Bent over, your hands on my hips,

teeth grazing my neck,

dick pressing, demanding, punishing, claiming.

I'm quivering, pussy soaked,

moaning your name.

Every slam, every want, every bite

drags me further—closer to collapse,

closer to you,

helpless, raw, surrendered.

"Beg for it," you command,

and I do,

taking you deep,

trying to throw it back,

needing every inch, every thrust,

but I can't.

My body is screaming for your dominance.

You have no problem pinning me down,

making me helpless.

I am yours—completely, unapologetically,

tongue-tied,

every nerve screaming for your control,

every gasp a relinquish,

every moan a confession

that you own me—body and soul—

and I would take it endlessly,

consumed by your fire,

ruined and alive in your demand and desire.

I want it all—every savage claim, every brutal thrust,

every inch of you buried deep inside me,

ravished,

uncontrollable jerks,

hanging on the edge of losing myself completely,

because you're untamable, ruthless,

and I don't want to survive it; I want it,

all of it,

again and again until there's nothing left of me,

only your debris.

Whisper My Name

Your breath is fire on my skin,

lips grazing, teeth teasing,

tongue tracing every line,

every curve, every sensitive fold

that begs for attention.

I shiver, gasp,

heart pounding, body trembling,

lost in the slow, deliberate rhythm

of your hands, your mouth, your fingers

dragging me toward a heat I cannot resist.

Whisper my name,

and I melt,

dripping,

burning,

every nerve alive with want,

every inch of me aching for you.

FUCK! I want you.

Your touch is possession,

claiming,

consuming,

fingers and lips AND that tongue

mapping me like I'm yours to explore,

pushing me further, higher,

to the edge I thought I could hold

but cannot.

I scream, whimper, and gasp,

your name tangled in mine,

your body sliding into me,

every thrust, every slick press, every drag

igniting a storm that leaves me raw,

hungry, trembling.

I'm yours, completely,

lost in the fire of your mouth,

the grip of your hands,

the madness of your body,

and I will take it, every inch,

every taste, every delicious, sinful moment

until I cannot hold myself together

NATALYA

because I am undone.

I'm about to cum!

Uhhh. That dick!

After Midnight

We're home after a night of laughter and drinks,

but the party hasn't left us.

A shot, a pour of wine,

your favorite drink waiting—Cuervo, chilled, salted rim.

The fireplace crackles,

music hums low from the TV.

We talk, we laugh,

but then our mouths find each other,

soft at first, then complete desire.

We want it all,

pushing the moment to the edge,

watching, letting ourselves be seen,

the Airplay reflecting every naughty smile,

every playful touch.

Your kiss deepens, intense.

My body responds,

wet and giving in,

hands roaming, mouths tasting,

NATALYA

eyes locking as we see ourselves

on the screen and in each other.

My mouth finds you;

you give me a taste test.

You can't resist;

I can't either.

You turn me over and align yourself

between my legs

and take me slow, relentless,

filling me,

making me yours.

Every touch, every thrust, every grasp,

sweet, erotic,

until all that's left

is us—

making love in the still of the night

while the world is asleep.

Velvet Heat

Every glance, every brush of your hand

ignites a fire I keep just for you.

Role play with your man.

A lady in the streets,

a bitch in his sheets.

Be his fantasy.

Buy the vibrating panties.

Let him hold the remote.

Set it on soft—

just enough to stir you,

to tease him without giving it all away.

Aroused, but subtle.

Silent electricity humming between you.

Let your eyes speak first—

a slow, knowing look,

that heat behind your gaze that makes him ache.

The way you walk, the sway of your hips,

every glance a promise of what's to come.

NATALYA

In public, polite, composed.

Behind closed doors, wild, unrestrained, hungry.

His mind remembers when you whisper his name, moan into his ear,

and he can taste the fire you keep just for him.

His soldier, a prelude to attention,

a teasing spark, a delicious pre-taste.

Tease. Tempt. Tantalize.

Be the woman he can't stop thinking about—

the fantasy he never wants to end.

Control in his hands,

pleasure in yours.

Desire unleashed,

slow burn turning into pure, heated chaos.

Tell him you can't hold it any longer.

Text him: I need you, baby!

He sees the desire, the hunger in you,

and suddenly control isn't optional.

In the bathroom,

hands on the sink,

you arch, pressing closer.

His lips find yours, demanding—

no, insistent.

Tongues dancing, teeth grazing,

fire spilling through every touch.

Your nails trace his back;

his hands grip your hips,

every movement claiming, devouring.

He feels the vibration between your legs,

singing your secret.

He fucks you against the cool tile,

pulling you hard, deep, relentless.

Every gasp, every tremor,

every curve pressed to his body

is a promise of the night ahead,

your moans echoing in the heat of the room.

His lady.

His bitch.

His fantasy.

His.

Boundaries

Why do men say they want a good woman

until they actually get one,

and suddenly they don't know what the fuck to do with her?

I don't play games.

I don't give halfway love.

Everything I do is 100%—no in-between.

When I love, I give my body, my time, my soul.

I don't hold back.

I cook.

I nurture.

I listen.

I support.

I fuck with fire.

Kiss with hunger.

Touch like I'm claiming every inch of you.

I make sure my man feels like a King—

inside and out.

I'm as real as they come.

And, somehow, that makes men think they can take advantage.

My devotion isn't an invitation.

It isn't a welcome mat.

Nights turn into excuses.

He goes out with his boys.

I wait.

Burning.

Anticipating.

Midnight.

Two a.m.

The sun rises.

No call.

No text.

No explanation.

Sometimes he doesn't come home the next night either.

And when he finally crawls into bed,

smelling like liquor—

and someone else's perfume—

what am I supposed to do?

Smile?

NATALYA

Pretend everything is fine?

Where the fuck do they learn that?

All I ever wanted was simple:

A love built on loyalty.

A man who chooses me

the way I choose him.

To travel.

Laugh.

Fuck until the headboard breaks.

Explore every curve.

Moan with intent.

Build a life where we feed each other—in every way.

Live fully until God calls us home.

But, apparently, that's too much to ask.

So, now I'm done.

Done being a pushover.

Done pretending my pleasure comes second.

Boundaries? Oh, I've got them.

I'm laying bricks—strong, unshakable.

The first one is this:

I am number one.

If I don't like it, it's not happening.

If my body isn't on fire, I'm not faking it.

If my spirit feels uneasy, I won't ignore it.

If a man can't bring me to my knees with passion,

love me with devotion,

worship every part of me—the way I deserve—

he can step aside.

I may have been too much for him.

But I will never not be enough for me.

Sneak Peak

Sitting me on his lap and prying my legs open he whispered, *"Just a little bit,"* as he reached for my young pussy while he smelled his fingers and jerked his old ass dick off. I had no idea what the fuck was happening. I knew I wasn't supposed to be doing that or with him. It changed my innocence. Some people become resentful and grow up all negative and shit. My life went another route, but I was too embarrassed to admit it. Every so often, that thought creeps in my head. *Motherfucker. I hope you rot in hell.* I got myself together and jumped in the shower. I was meeting up with one of my best friends, Tashanyk—who we call Nyk for short—to have some drinks. I'd had a crazy week and needed it.

Music was lit and there were a few people in there; I mean brothers. We get to the bar and, immediately, someone sends us drinks. *"Ah, hell, here we go,"* Nyk said. We knew it would be a short time before he came our way. The nigga looked familiar. We smiled simultaneously. He sat and we chatted. I bought him a drink back. Conversation was great, and by the end of the night, we exchanged numbers ...

~ Coming soon!

ABOUT THE AUTHOR

Natalya writes from the heart—with ink made of memory, desire, shared stories, and reflection. Her work draws from real-life moments and the emotional weight of what's felt but rarely said aloud. Through poetry and storytelling, she explores the raw edges of love, loss, healing, and human connection.

A passionate creator and founder of *Natalya Writes Publishing*, Natalya inspires readers with her authenticity, vulnerability, and unfiltered truth—one page at a time.

A quiet observer and soulful storyteller, Natalya invites readers to see themselves in her words—to feel seen, heard, and understood. Her writing is honest yet intentional, sensual yet grounded, and always deeply human—a voice for the brave women who shared their stories.

www.ingramcontent.com/pod-product-compliance
Lightning Source LLC
Chambersburg PA
CBHW060314310726
48976CB00007B/2320